W9-DAE-922

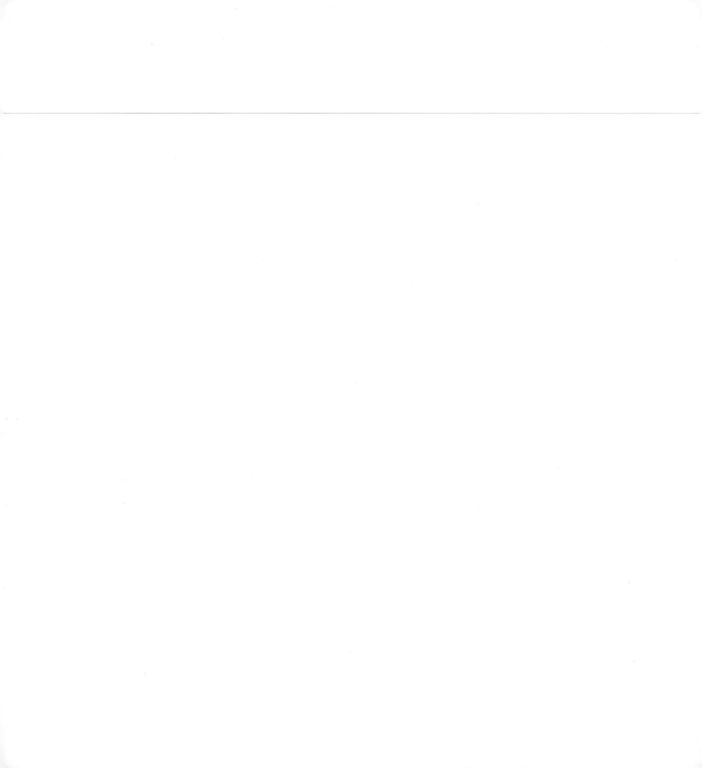

New Jersey
The Garden State

Tika Downey

PowerKiDS press™

New York

Published in 2010 by The Rosen Publishing Group, Inc.
29 East 21st Street, New York, NY 10010

First Edition

Editor: Joanne Randolph
Book Design: Greg Tucker
Layout Design: Kate Laczynski
Photo Researcher: Jessica Gerweck

Photo Credits: Cover © Super Stock/age fotostock; pp. 5, 9 © www.istockphoto.com/Andrew F. Kazmierski; p. 7 MPI/Getty Images; p. 11 © www.istockphoto.com/John Mroz; pp. 13, 15, 17, 22 (animal, flower) Shutterstock.com; p. 19 © www.istockphoto.com/Sterling Stevens; p. 22 (bird) © www.istockphoto.com/Frank Leung; p. 22 (tree) © www.istockphoto.com/Roger Whiteway; p. 22 (Buzz Aldrin) Mark Wilson/Getty Images; p. 22 (Judy Blume) Evan Agostini/Getty Images; p. 22 (Kevin Jonas) Carlos Alvarez/Getty Images.

Library of Congress Cataloging-in-Publication Data

Downey, Tika.
  New Jersey : the Garden State / Tika Downey. — 1st ed.
      p. cm. — (Our amazing states)
  Includes index.
  ISBN 978-1-4358-9355-9 (library binding) — ISBN 978-1-4358-9806-6 (pbk.) —
ISBN 978-1-4358-9807-3 (6-pack)
  1. New Jersey—Juvenile literature. I. Title.
  F134.3.D69 2010
  974.9—dc22

                                   2009029084

Manufactured in the United States of America

CPSIA Compliance Information: Batch #WW10PK: For Further Information contact Rosen Publishing, New York, New York at 1-800-237-9932

Contents

The Garden State

Did you know that New Jersey was one of the original 13 states? In fact, it was the third state to join the nation. It is located along the Atlantic coast, with New York to the north and Pennsylvania to the west. Because of its position, more battles were fought in New Jersey during the **American Revolution** than in any other state.

Today, New Jersey has more people than 39 other states, even though it is one of the smallest states. People often picture crowded cities and factories when they think of New Jersey. However, it is famous for its beaches and farms, too. In fact, it is called the Garden State because it grows so many fruits, vegetables, and other plants on its farms.

4

New Jersey is famous for the many beaches along its shore. The Jersey Shore is 127 miles (204 km) long and brings many visitors to New Jersey.

A Journey Through New Jersey's Past

New Jersey's first people arrived about 10,000 years ago. They called themselves the Lenape, which means "people" or "true people." Later European settlers called them the Delaware Indians.

Giovanni da Verrazano, an Italian explorer, was likely the first European to see New Jersey in 1524. Dutch settlers built the first lasting European colony there in 1660, but the English took control in 1664.

During the American Revolution, about 100 battles were fought in New Jersey. Three of the chief ones were at Trenton, Princeton, and Monmouth. New Jersey factories helped the colonies win the war by making supplies for the soldiers. New Jersey became a state in 1787.

Here Washington leads soldiers in the Battle of Princeton, which was fought on January 3, 1777. The Americans won the battle.

Monmouth Battlefield State Park

Do you like to visit famous historic places? Monmouth Battlefield State Park is a good place to visit in New Jersey. On June 28, 1778, the longest and largest **artillery** land battle of the American Revolution happened there.

General George Washington, who was the leader of the American forces, and his soldiers fought British soldiers on June 28. Washington planned to attack again the next morning, but the British left during the night. The Americans had won the last big battle fought in the northern colonies.

Today you can learn about the battle at the park's visitor center. If you visit in late June, you may get to see a **reenactment** of the battle!

This is the Sutfin Farmhouse, which you can see if you visit Monmouth Battlefield State Park. The Battle of Monmouth Courthouse took place on June 28, 1778.

Weather and Geography in New Jersey

New Jersey has cold winters and warm summers. However, ocean winds make summers cooler and winters warmer along the coast.

New Jersey's **geography** has mountains, including High Point, the state's tallest mountain at 1,803 feet (550 m) in the north. It also has cliffs called the Palisades along the Hudson River. Great **Swamp** National Wildlife **Refuge**, South Mountain Reservation, and most of New Jersey's rivers are in the north, too, including the Hudson, Delaware, Passaic, Raritan, and Hackensack.

The Atlantic Coastal Plain covers southern New Jersey. The western plain is good for farming, but the eastern plain has poor, sandy soil.

The Pine Barrens, a heavily forested area, is found on New Jersey's Atlantic Coastal Plain. A barren is a flat place where not many plants grow.

Natural New Jersey

Do you picture factories when you think of New Jersey? Well, guess what? Forests cover almost half the state! The state flower, the violet, grows throughout the forests. New Jersey even has plants, such as the purple pitcher plant, that eat bugs!

Animals such as bears, deer, foxes, opossums, raccoons, turtles, and snakes live in New Jersey. The coastal waters have clams, crabs, and lobsters. There are many kinds of birds, too. A colorful one is the goldfinch, the state bird of New Jersey.

Goldfinches are small songbirds. Females are greenish brown, but males are bright yellow, with a black cap, wings, and tail. Goldfinches eat mostly small seeds.

Because of goldfinches' beautiful song and the males' bright color, people often call them wild canaries.

Factories and Farms in the Garden State

Many U.S. companies and companies from other countries have factories in New Jersey. **Chemical** goods, especially **medicines**, are the main **products** made there. Other major chemical products include shampoo, lotion, and perfume. New Jersey factories also make food products. You might have eaten baked goods or canned fruits and vegetables from New Jersey!

Remember, though, that New Jersey got its nickname, the Garden State, because plants grow well there. Do you like peaches, blueberries, corn, or squash? You might have had some that were grown in New Jersey! The state's farmers also grow spinach, wheat, hay, and many other crops.

Farming has long been an important business in New Jersey. The Historic Long Street Farm, in Holmdel, gives visitors a look at 1890s farm life.

Let's Talk About Trenton

Trenton began as a Quaker settlement in 1679. In 1714, William Trent bought part of the settlement. It was named Trent's Town, which later became Trenton, in his honor. It was picked as New Jersey's capital in 1790.

You can still see William Trent's house today. You can also see the government at work in the statehouse, which has a gold **dome** on top. What else can you do in Trenton? You can learn about the state's past at the New Jersey State **Museum**. You can go to the Douglass House, which George Washington used during the American Revolution. You can learn about science, too, at the Invention Factory Science Center. There is a lot to do in Trenton!

New Jersey's statehouse, in Trenton, was built in 1792. Trenton was the U.S. capital twice, once in 1784 and again in 1792!

Colorful Cape May

Cape May, at New Jersey's southern tip, is the nation's oldest beach **resort**. It is especially famous for two things, the nearby lighthouse and the city's old, colorfully painted homes. The first lighthouse was built in 1823. The one there now was built in 1859 and is still working. You can visit it and climb the stairs to the top or see the keeper's house, which was built in 1860.

Fire destroyed Cape May City in 1878, but the people soon rebuilt it. The new houses were built in what is called the Victorian style. No other place in the country has so many Victorian homes. Cape May is also known for its birds. Hundreds of people visit Cape May's many bird-watching hot spots each year.

Cape May Lighthouse looks out over Delaware Bay and the Atlantic Ocean. The light can be seen 24 miles (39 km) out to sea and flashes every 15 seconds.

A Guide to the Garden State

Whatever you like to do for fun, you can find it in the Garden State. Every year, millions of people visit. Many go to coastal resorts, where they swim in the Atlantic Ocean, play on the beaches, go shopping, or visit museums. Some visit Atlantic City's **casinos**.

Others like to hike along the Palisades. Some enjoy bird-watching at Great Swamp National Wildlife Refuge, South Mountain Reservation, and Cape May. Others like to visit historic places such as Monmouth Battlefield State Park and Morristown National Historical Park. George Washington and his soldiers stayed at Morristown during the hard winter of 1779 to 1780. Many people enjoy the cities. What would you like to do in New Jersey?

Glossary

American Revolution (uh-MER-uh-ken reh-vuh-LOO-shun) Battles that soldiers from the colonies fought against Britain for freedom, from 1775 to 1783.

artillery (ahr-TIH-lur-ee) The part of the army that uses large guns, such as cannons.

casinos (kuh-SEE-nohz) Places where people play games of chance for money.

chemical (KEH-mih-kul) Matter that can be mixed with other matter to cause changes.

dome (DOHM) A type of curved roof.

geography (jee-AH-gruh-fee) The features of the land in a place.

medicines (MEH-duh-sinz) Drugs that a doctor gives you to help fight illness.

museum (myoo-ZEE-um) A place where art or historical pieces are safely kept for people to see and to study.

products (PRAH-dukts) Things that are produced.

reenactment (ree-uh-NAKT-ment) Something that is relived, or done again.

refuge (REH-fyooj) A place that gives shelter or security.

resort (rih-ZORT) A place people go to have fun and relax.

swamp (SWOMP) A wet land with a lot of trees and bushes.

New Jersey State Symbols

State Tree
Red Oak

State Animal
Horse

State Flag

State Bird
Eastern Goldfinch

State Flower
Common Violet

State Seal

Famous People from New Jersey

Edwin "Buzz" Aldrin
(1930–)
Born in Montclair, NJ
Astronaut

Judy Blume
(1938–)
Born in Elizabeth, NJ
Author

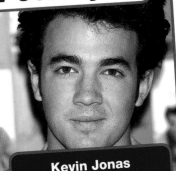
Kevin Jonas
(1987–)
Born in Teaneck, NJ
Singer/Actor

New Jersey State Map

High Point
Lake Mohawk
Lake Hopatcong
Hudson River
Passaic River
Paramus
Paterson
Passaic
Hackensack
Hoboken
Newark
Jersey City
Elizabeth
Woodbridge
Edison
Raritan River
Princeton
Monmouth
⭐ Trenton
Delaware River
Camden
Mullica River
Maurice River
Atlantic City
Great Egg Harbor
Cape May

Legend

○ Major City

⭐ Capital

〜 River

New Jersey State Facts

Nickname: The Garden State

Population: 8,682,661

Area: About 7,787 square miles (20,168 sq km)

Motto: "Liberty and Prosperity"

Song: Unofficial song is "I'm from New Jersey," words and music by Red Mascara

Index

Web Sites

Due to the changing nature of Internet links, PowerKids Press has developed an online list of Web sites related to the subject of this book. This site is updated regularly. Please use this link to access the list:
www.powerkidslinks.com/amst/nj/